DRAGONS LOVE TACOS

by Adam Rubin
illustrated by Daniel Salmieri

SCHOLASTIC INC.

ISBN 978-0-545-60426-0

Text copyright © 2012 by Adam Rubin.
Illustrations copyright © 2012 by Daniel Salmieri.
All rights reserved. Published by Scholastic Inc.,
557 Broadway, New York, NY 10012,
by arrangement with Dial Books for Young Readers,
a division of Penguin Young Readers Group,
a member of Penguin Group (USA) Inc.
SCHOLASTIC and associated logos are trademarks
and/or registered trademarks of Scholastic Inc.

21   20 21 22/0

Printed in the U.S.A.   40

First Scholastic printing, September 2013

Designed by Jennifer Kelly
Text set in Zemke Hand ITC Std
The artwork was created with watercolor, gouache, and color pencil.

Hey, kid!
Did you know that dragons love tacos?
They love beef tacos and chicken tacos.
They love really big gigantic tacos and tiny
little baby tacos as well.

Why do dragons love tacos?

Maybe it's the smell from the sizzling pan.

Maybe it's the crunch of the crispy tortillas.

Maybe it's a secret.

Either way, if you want to make friends with dragons, tacos are key.

Hey dragon, why do you guys love tacos so much?

But wait!

As much as dragons love tacos, they hate spicy salsa even more.

They hate spicy green salsa and spicy red salsa.

They hate spicy chunky salsa and spicy smooth salsa.

If the salsa is spicy at all, dragons can't stand it.

ORLA'S SPICY SALSA

Why do dragons hate spicy salsa?
Well, just one drop of hot sauce
makes a dragon's ears smoke.

Just one single speck of hot pepper makes a dragon snort sparks.
Spicy salsa gives dragons the tummy troubles,
and when dragons get the tummy troubles—
oh boy . . .

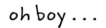

If you want to make tacos for dragons, keep the toppings mild.

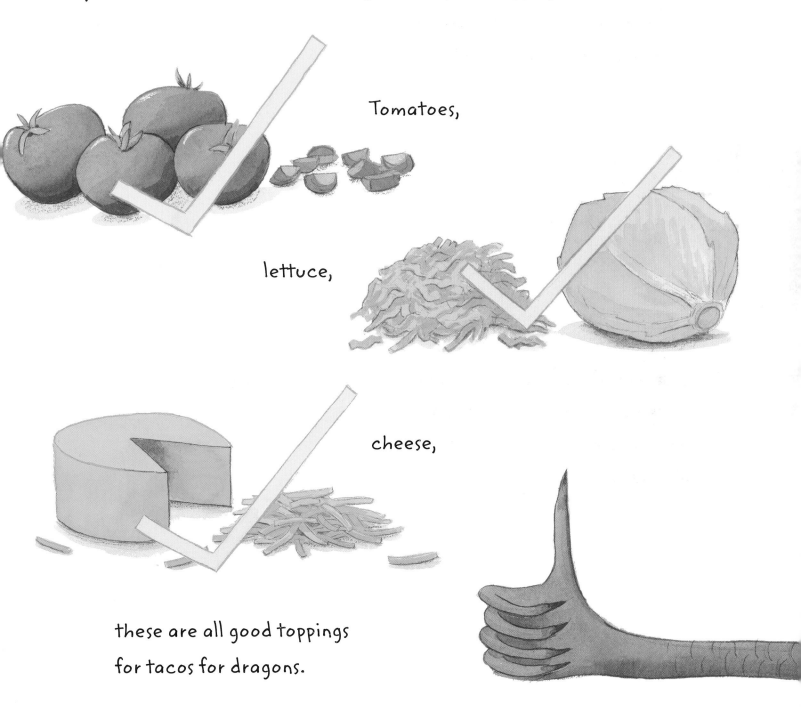

Tomatoes,

lettuce,

cheese,

these are all good toppings
for tacos for dragons.

Hey dragon, how do you feel about spicy taco toppings?

Dragons love parties. They like costume parties

and pool parties.

They like big gigantic parties with accordions

and tiny little parties with charades.

Why do dragons love parties? Maybe it's the conversation. Maybe it's the dancing. Maybe it's the comforting sound of a good friend's laughter.

The only thing dragons love more than parties or tacos, is taco parties (taco parties are parties with lots of tacos).

If you want to have some dragons over for a taco party, you'll need buckets of tacos. Pantloads of tacos. The best way to judge is to get a boat and fill the boat with tacos. That's about how many tacos dragons need for a taco party. After all, dragons love tacos.

Hey dragon, are you excited for the big taco party?

Just remember: Dragons hate spicy salsa.
Before you host your taco party with dragons,
get rid of all the spicy salsa. In fact, bury the spicy
salsa in the backyard so the dragons can't find it.

These dragons love your taco party! They love the music.
They love the decorations. They especially love the tacos.

Congratulations!

It's a good thing you got rid of all that spicy . . .

Wait a second—

what are those little green things in the salsa?
You didn't read the fine print?!

Dragons, listen to me: Do not eat those tacos.
Those little green specs in the salsa? Those are jalapeño peppers—
they are super-spicy! I know you love tacos, dragons, but you are
not gonna love those tacos.

DO NOT LET THOSE DRAGONS EAT THOSE TACOS!!!

Crunch, crunch, crunch . . .

Too late . . .

Why would dragons help you rebuild your house?

Maybe they're good Samaritans.

Maybe they feel bad for wrecking it.

Maybe they're just in it for the taco breaks.

After all, dragons love tacos.